A Look at the Calendar

Sharon Moore

Rosen REAL READERS

I0809726

Rosen Classroom Books & Materials
New York

April days of the week

Sunday	Monday	Tuesday	Wednesday	Thursday	Friday	Saturday
	2	3	4	5	6	7
8	9	10	11	12	13	14
15	16	17	18	19	20	21
22	23	24	25	26	27	28
29	30					

A **calendar** shows us the days of the week. There are seven days in a week.

A calendar shows us the **months** of the **year**. There are twelve months in a year.

Sunday	Monday	Tuesday	Wednesday	Thursday	Friday	Saturday
1	2	3	4	5	6	7
8	9	10	11	12	13	14
15	16	17	18	19	20	21
22	23	24	25	26	27	28
29	30					

Sunday	Monday	Tuesday	Wednesday	Thursday	Friday	Saturday
		1	2	3	4	5
6	7	8	9	10	11	12
13	14	15	16	17	18	19
20	21	22	23	24	25	26
27	28	29	30	31		

A calendar shows us how many days are in a month. Most months have 30 or 31 days.

April						
Sunday	Monday	Tuesday	Wednesday	Thursday	Friday	Saturday
1	2	3	4	5	6	7
8	9	10	11	12 My Birthday	13	14
15	16			9	20	21
22	23			6	27	28
29	30					

A calendar helps us remember important **dates** like birthdays.

Do you want to find out what day your birthday is this year? Look at a calendar.

month

April						
Sunday	Monday	Tuesday	Wednesday	Thursday	Friday	Saturday
1	2	3	4	5	6	7
8	9	10	11	12	13	14
15	16	17	18	19	20	21
22	23	24	25	26	27	28
29	30					

First find the month of your birthday on the calendar. **April** is the name of this month.

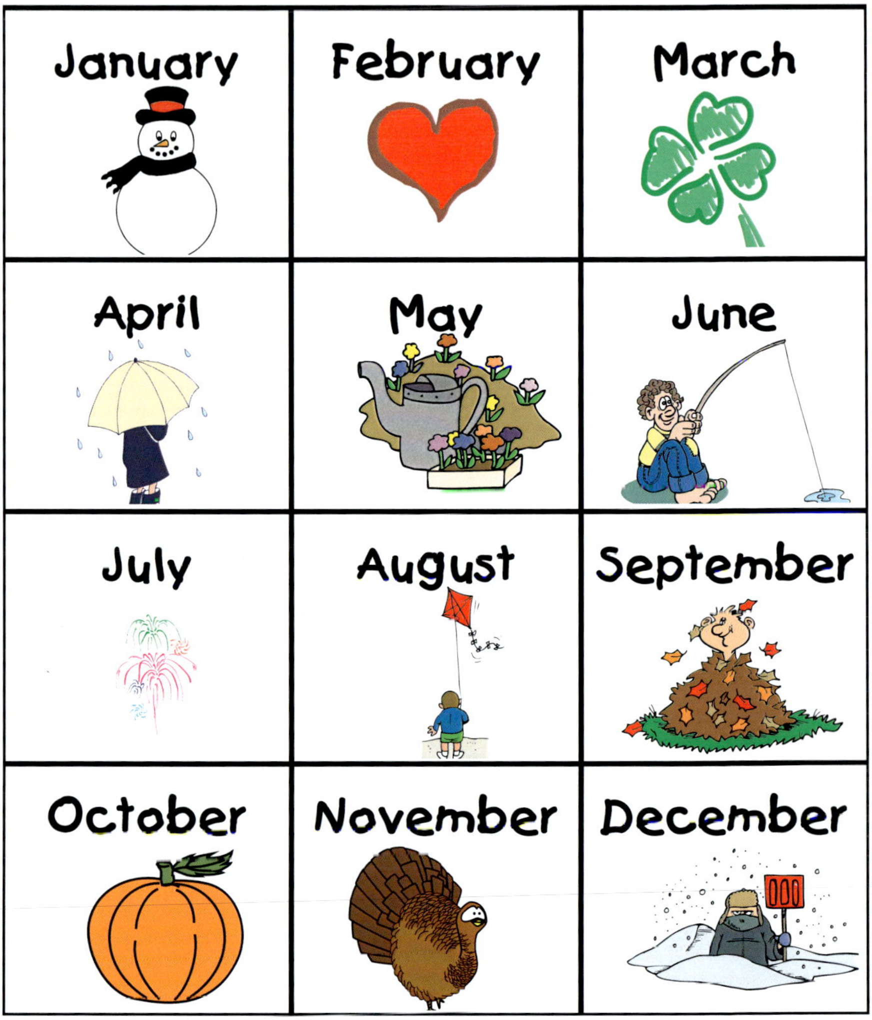

Is your birthday in April or
another month?

month

date

April						
Sunday	Monday	Tuesday	Wednesday	Thursday	Friday	Saturday
1	2	3	4	5	6	7
8	9	10	11	12	13	14
15	16	17	18	19	20	21
22	23	24	25	26	27	28
29	30					

What is the date of your birthday? Can you find it on a calendar?

month

day

April						
Sunday	Monday	Tuesday	Wednesday	Thursday	Friday	Saturday
1	2	3	4	5	6	7
8	9	10	11	12	13	14
15	16	17	18	19	20	21
22	23	24	25	26	27	28
29	30					

Is your birthday on a Sunday, Monday, or another day this year?

Now you can mark the day of your birthday on the calendar!

Glossary

April The fourth month of the year.

calendar A chart showing the days, weeks, and months of the year.

date Any one day. April 12 is a date.

month A part of the year. There are twelve months in a year.

year An amount of time that lasts for 12 months or 365 days.